BILL AND THE FISH
(i as in sit and ll as in fill)

"Bill see, there's a pink
fish in the pit," cried Jill.

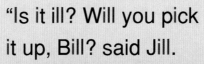

"Is it ill? Will you pick
it up, Bill? said Jill.

"I will fill a bit of water in this tin dish and dip the fish in it", said Jill.
"Grip it well or it will slip, Bill.

It fits well. Give it some
biscuit. See it lick!

4

It spins and flicks its fin.

Now it seems
fit to do a Jig!!

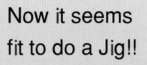

OLD MONDY MOLE
(o as in hole)

Mondy Mole walked along the road which was covered
with snow.
He was pushing his wheelbarrow
full of toads to be sold.

He was growing old and so felt very cold.
He wore a coat and over it, an overcoat,
yet his throat was hoarse due to cold.

As he reached the shore, he
saw the steamboat float away.
Low in spirit, Mondy Mole sat
down near a pole. His toes hurt.

Just then, Jolly Goat rode by on her favourite Joan, the Foal.

She said to Mondy Mole, "Grandpa, don't lose hope. We will race along the shore and catch the steamboat at the port.

Mondy Mole rose. His spirit soared and off he went with the dear Jolly Goat.

BRAVE HEART MARCUS
(a as in arm and rk as in park)

Mark is a retired army man.
He now lives on a farm.
He starts his task very early
in the morning

His son, Marcus loves to bask on the calm beach with lots of palm trees.

He hunts sharks with darts and a harpoon.

Once, a shark charged at him
but Marcus was not alarmed.
He has a big scar on his arm
but Marcus is a brave heart.

Marcus is now a famous artist who paints on
the barks of trees in the park, near the market.

He is also a pop star who sings
and plays the guitar and the harp.
Marcus has won everyone's hearts.

MR. CRUNCH THE BUFFALO
(ch as in church and u as in bun)

Mr. Crunch the Buffalo waited for the bus with a bundle of grass to munch. He was very cheerful for he was going to meet his chum, Mr. Dumb, the Buck, for lunch.

What fun I will have with my childhood buddy—humming in the sun and playing the drums, thought Mr. Crunch.

Just then, Mr. Jump, the
Bug and Miss Cherrie, the
Bumblebee whizzed past him
and bumped into a branch.

All the chestnuts which Mr. Jump
carried fell into the mud.
"How clumsy you are!" cried
Miss Cherrie, the Bumblebee.

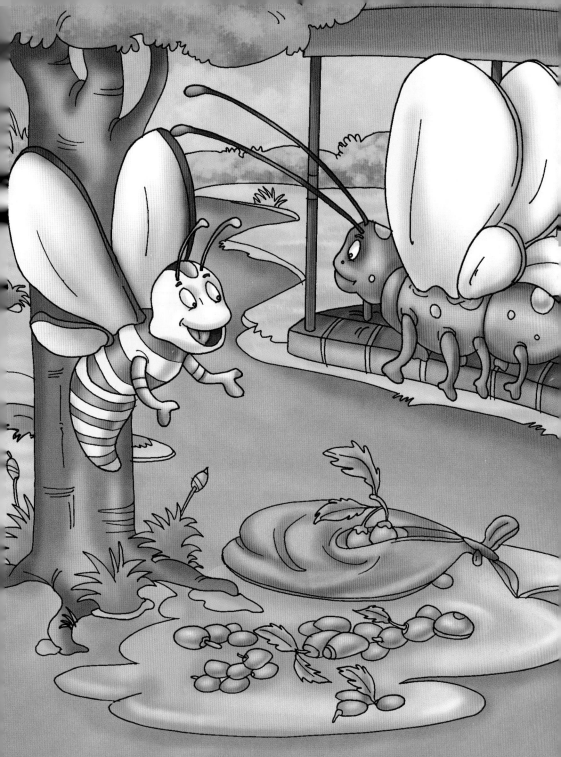

Mr. Jump, the Bug blushed and looked
very glum. He mumbled," Miss Cherrie,
I am sorry. It was a blunder."

"Oh, don't worry, dear Miss Cherrie. I have a cheese and honey sandwich which both of us will eat, sitting on the rug with a mug of chilled chocolate shake.